# STORM RESCUE

Adaptation from the animated series: Anne Paradis
Illustrations: ROI VISUAL

## CRACKBOOM!

A lightning storm is brewing in Broomstown.

The Robocar rescue team goes out on patrol to help citizens be prepared and stay safe.

Helly sets up a lightning rod as Mini, Benny and Rody watch curiously.
"The lightning rod is a stick that protects you from lightning."

"Is lightning dangerous?" Mini asks.
"Yes, very!" Helly replies. "Lightning can start fires and cause a lot of damage."

When Helly's gone, the three friends talk about the coming storm. "Do you know how lightning is made?" Rody asks.

"Yes!" says Mini. "It's when the clouds crash together in the sky and go BOOM!"
"That's not right!" cries Benny. "I heard that lightning strikes when the sky is angry."

"Don't be silly!" says Rody. "Lightning happens when sky giants do battle. Their spears are made of lightning, and when they hit each other, it goes BOOM!"

The three friends decide to go up to the highest point in the whole town to see the lightning up close and find out who's right.

Meanwhile, Jin reveals her invention: a lightning-defense shield.

"That's amazing!" Roy says. "With this shield, I'd feel safe going on a rescue mission even in stormy weather!"

Poli volunteers to try out the shield. Jin installs the lightning-protection chip in his system.
"Defense shield, GO!" Poli says.
Jin fires a lightning bolt to test the shield. The lightning strikes, but Poli can't feel it. It's awesome!

Mini, Benny and Rody make their way to the very top of town. Suddenly, the sky grows dark and it starts to rain. Mini and Benny get a little worried.

"Hurry up! We're almost there," Rody says.

At the top of Galaxy Hill, it's raining even harder.

"I should never have come here!" Mini complains. "It's cold and I'm scared!"
"Come on, let's go wait in that cave until the lightning starts," says Rody.
Once they're inside the cave, the three friends feel a little safer.

**Yahoo !**

Suddenly, the thunder and lightning begin.
"The sky giants are doing battle! Let's go see!" Rody cries in excitement.
But Mini and Benny don't want to go back outside the cave. They are scared.

"Well, fine, I'll go outside and see the lightning without you!" says Rody, leaving them inside the cave.

**Bang !**

Lightning strikes the cave entrance and causes a rock slide.
"Rody, help us! We can't get out!"
Mini and Benny shout.
The rocks are far too big for Rody to move. He needs to get help—and fast!

Rody calls Rescue Team
Headquarters to get help for
Mini and Benny.

Poli, Roy, Amber and Helly come to the rescue right away!

The storm is raging. Helly
helps Rody find shelter.

"Poli, it's too dangerous to move these rocks
during the storm," Roy says.
"The lightning shield will keep me safe,
and I'll use a lightning rod to protect you,"
Poli replies.

Poli climbs to the top of the hill and activates the shield. Then he holds up a lightning rod to catch the lightning.

"Roy! Amber! Go now and be quick—I don't know how long the shield will hold!"
Roy and Amber rush over to the cave entrance.

Roy and Amber start moving the rocks.
They can hear Mini and Benny shouting
for help.

"The rescue team is here! Don't be scared, kids," Amber says.
"We'll get you out of there!"
Together they push the big boulder away from the entrance.

Mini and Benny hurry out of the cave under Amber and Roy's protection. Phew! Just in time! Poli's shield is about to give out.

Poli jumps down from the top of the hill and moves quickly away from the lightning that is striking the rocks.

"Kids, you could have been seriously hurt," Amber says, once they are all safely inside. "It's very dangerous to go out alone in weather like this, and you should never try to get close to lightning." Mini, Benny and Rody feel bad.

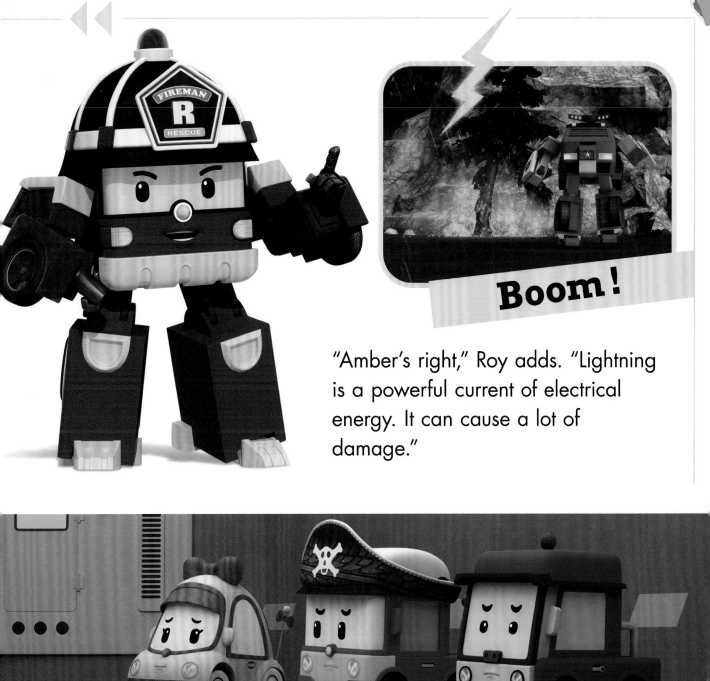

**Boom!**

"Amber's right," Roy adds. "Lightning is a powerful current of electrical energy. It can cause a lot of damage."

"So, lightning is just electrical energy? But where does it come from?" asks Rody curiously.

"Air particles in clouds have electric charges," Amber explains.

"During a storm, the clouds bump into each other. That creates a big spark of electricity and makes a big thundering sound."

"I knew I was right," says Mini proudly.

"Next time you're curious about the weather, don't go exploring alone. Ask an adult to explain it instead," Poli reminds them.
"We promise, Poli!" the kids reply.

Jin calls the Robocar rescue team to tell them the storm is over.

**It's time to go back to headquarters!**

CrackBoom! Books is an imprint of Chouette Publishing (1987) Inc.

Text: adaptation by Anne Paradis of the animated series Robocar Poli, produced by ROI Visual.
All rights reserved.
Original script written by Ji Min AHN
Original episode #418: Boom! Crash! Danger!

Illustrations:  © ROI VISUAL / EBS All rights reserved.

Chouette Publishing would like to thank the Government of Canada and SODEC
for their financial support.

Québec ✚✚
Books          Gestion
Tax Credit     SODEC

Bibliothèque et Archives nationales du Québec and Library and Archives
Canada cataloguing in publication

Paradis, Anne 1972-,

[Sauvetage éclair. English]
Storm rescue/text, Anne Paradis; illustrations, Roi Visual; translation,
David Warriner.

(Robocar Poli)
(CrackBoom! Books)
Translation of: Sauvetage éclair.

Target audience: For children aged 3 and up.

ISBN 978-2-924786-86-4 (softcover)

I. Warriner, David, translator. II. Roi Visual (Firm), illustrator. III. Title.
IV. Title: Sauvetage éclair. English.

PS8631.A713S2813 2018        j843'.6        C2018-941657-2
PS9631.A713S2813 2018

Printed in Canada
10 9 8 7 6 5 4 3 2 1   CHO2043 AUG2018